Kindness Grows

by Britta Teckentrup

To Pat and Tom
~ Britta

tiger tales

It all
    starts
        with a
            crack
        that we can hardly see.

It happens when we shout

                or if we disagree.

But
with
every
kindness
that we care to show,

something good and beautiful

will begin to grow.

Friendships can be damaged
by a mean
or ugly word.

Once it has been spoken,
it cannot be unheard.

Words of encouragement,
sweetness,
warmth,
and care,

blossom, grow, and flourish
as they spread love everywhere.

If we leave friends out,
        sad, and on their own,

            soon the crack will widen,

                and we'll be left alone.

Sharing things with others,
making a new friend,

will begin a journey

we hope will never end.

It's so hard to be friendly
when all we feel is sad.

Sometimes we are thoughtless,
and we make others feel bad.

But a kindly thought or action
can make somebody's day.

If we keep our friends close by,
we won't drive them away.

When we argue with each other

or we refuse to share,

the crack grows even wider,
but we don't know that it's there.

Playing all together

is always much more fun.

We have a lot of space here
for each and everyone!

Sometimes we are selfish.

We shout and stamp our feet,
        feeling annoyed and angry
                with everyone we meet.

But when we work together,

just look at what we can do!
Anything is possible,
when one plus one makes two.

Anger can consume us until we just can't see

the beauty that's around us—
the moon, the stars, a tree . . .

If we lean on one another,

and keep our friends around,
we make each other happy, warm and safe and sound.

The crack has grown so wide now—
can we ever make things right?

If we reach out to others,
then maybe we just might . . .

It only takes a gesture—
a smile can be the start

to spread the seed of friendship
and touch somebody's heart.

Reaching out to others
is not as difficult as it seems.

If we all join together,
  we can chase our dreams.

Our tree will
grow much stronger

the more we show
we care,

built from
love and kindness

and the friendships
that we share.